★ PRINCESS ★
PROTECTION PROGRAM

Royalty UNDERCOVER

By Wendy Loggia

Based on "Princess Protection Program," Teleplay by Annie DeYoung

Based on the Story by David Morgasen and Annie DeYoung

DISNEP PRESS

New York

Printed in the United States of America
First Edition
1 3 5 7 9 10 8 6 4 2
Library of Congress Control Number on file.
ISBN 978-1-4231-2296-8

For more Disney Press fun, visit www.disneybooks.com
Visit DisneyChannel.com

Chapter 1

*T*he sky was an incredible shade of blue. Palm fronds swayed in the breeze. A calypso band played on a terrace. The air smelled of coconuts and chlorine and bougainvillea. And the most important decision hanging over a tankini-clad Carter Mason at this very moment was . . .

"Hmmm. Mango or raspberry. I'm thinking I'm gonna have to go with the mango, Ricky. I'm feeling a tropical vibe."

"Make that two, please," Queen Rosalinda chimed in. A huge straw hat shaded her face from the sun.

The two friends grinned at one another

as the uniformed palace waiter made a small bow. "Excellent choice." As Ricky walked back to the outside kitchen on the other side of the ornate lap pool, Carter let out a happy sigh.

"I still can't believe you get to live like this every day, Rosie. Like—like a queen!"

Rosie giggled. "I *am* the queen, Carter."

"And how awesome is that? You get your own private pool, cabanas, waiters who bring you whatever you want. . . . Now if only you could get the guys over there to play a little rock and roll, life would be perfect."

Rosie laughed again, bopping her head to the beat. "They're a calypso band, Carter. They're hoping for a slot in the Independence Day parade. This is a sort of audition for them."

"But what about a calypso band that plays Elvis? Or . . . or country? Or hip-hop?"

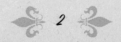

Carter's face lit up. "Now that would be something to listen to!"

"Add it to the list." Rosie waved her hand toward the thick stack of papers that sat on the small patio table between her and Carter. "Each time I cross one item off, I add two new ones. You should see what I have to accomplish tomorrow."

As queen, Rosalinda was in charge of planning the annual Costa Luna Independence Day celebration festivities. And from what Rosie had shared about her duties so far, it was no small job.

Carter slid her sunglasses down her nose and looked at Rosie over the rims. "How about having fun? That should go straight to the top. We've both been too stressed." She began ticking things off on her fingers. "You can't imagine how busy school has been. Three papers, five midterms, and two presentations . . . and that's just for English class."

When Rosie invited Carter to join her in Costa Luna for the Independence Day celebration, Carter had her bags packed within the hour. She wanted nothing more than to leave school and work behind for a week in the sun. But after her arrival the day before, Carter was beginning to realize that Rosie didn't have much time for fun. She didn't have much time for anything.

"Fun? Hmmm." Rosie tapped her chin with a polished red fingernail. "I think that comes somewhere after food-tasting and before music selection."

Ricky brought over the girls' mango smoothies and a large bowl of corn chips. He set them on a glass table between the two of them. "Enjoy," he said.

Carter took a sip of her smoothie as she thought about all that had gone on in the past few weeks. Sure, she had been really busy at school, and there seemed to be more

and more customers at her dad's business, Joe's Bait Shack, back in Lake Monroe, Louisiana. But it was nothing compared to what Rosie had been going through, she thought guiltily.

Although she was just "Rosie" to Carter and her father, the rest of the world knew her as Queen Rosalinda Marie Montoya Fiore of the principality of Costa Luna. She was a teenager in charge of a whole country!

Carter crunched into a chip. "Your subjects don't want a stressed-out queen, Rosie. They want someone chill and happy."

Rosie stirred her smoothie with a straw. "I know. It is just that I want to do a good job. The Costa Luna Independence Day celebration, the parade, the royal ball . . . it all falls on my shoulders."

"Can't your mom help you? I mean, you are the queen, Rosie. You could command her to, right?" Carter asked, only half joking.

"Yes, my mother is working very hard to make everything a success." Rosie's forehead creased with worry. "But this is my first real test now that I am queen. It is a big deal, Carter. For me, it is like being in charge of—of the Super Bowl. I want to prove to my people that I can handle these responsibilities and am worthy of their trust."

Carter sat back in her chair. She could understand how Rosie felt. "But you've got to let people help you, Rosie. Maybe I can do something. Like"—she gazed around the pool, her eyes landing on the palace waiters—"maybe helping the palace staff with their fashion sense. Because, to be honest? Kneesocks and long shorts are not a look that works."

"I am afraid I have—what is that expression your father uses? Oh, yes. Bigger fish to fry." Rosie lowered her voice. "Major Mason told you about Natalie, right?"

Carter nodded. Natalie de Rouen was a

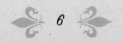

princess from Europe who was staying with Rosalinda in Costa Luna. Carter knew about Natalie because her father, Major Joe Mason, worked as an agent for the Princess Protection Program.

The Princess Protection Program was a top secret organization dedicated to keeping the princesses of the world safe. That was how Carter and Rosie had first met. Costa Luna had been threatened by a dictator, and Princess Rosalinda had been given a temporary new life as an average American teenager named Rosie González—until her country was secure and safe for her to return.

"Yeah, he did," Carter said. "My dad said her parents are getting a divorce and can't stop arguing over custody."

"Yes," Rosie said quietly. "There was concern that one of the de Rouens might abduct her. Your father and the Director

thought it best that Natalie be placed here under my supervision until custody arrangements can be amicably worked out."

Rosie reached into the tote bag by her chair and pulled out a photo of a blond girl, about nine years old. She was standing on a city street corner wearing a navy trench coat. Her hair was held back by a headband. She was frowning.

"Hmm. So what does Natalie look like now that she's had her makeover?" Carter asked, curious. The Princess Protection Program had four stages—and the third one was called transformation. "Does she have red hair now? Freckles? Cheaper-looking clothes?"

Rosie shook her head. "Because she is a child and her parents agreed to place her in the program, she didn't have to go through the four stages. Just Stage One—

extraction from her home—and Stage Four—relocation. She looks the same. Especially the frowning part."

"She doesn't want to be here, huh?" Carter asked.

Rosie shook her head. "And because of her situation, I have had to lie to the palace staff. Everyone believes Natalie is the daughter of dear family friends who are getting a divorce. They know she will be spending the next few weeks here, but they do not know she is really a princess. To them, she's just a little girl."

"Sounds familiar," Carter said, smiling as she thought back to when Rosie was undercover at her school. "And don't tell me—you're trying to teach her how to act like a regular girl?"

Rosie nodded. "Yes. And I am doing my best, but . . ." She let out a long, tired sigh. "I hate to say it, but she is very spoiled,

Carter. She is everything a princess should not be."

Carter studied the photo. "She's only nine, right? Bad habits should be pretty easy to break at her age."

"You have not met Natalie." Rosie turned in her lounge chair to face her friend. "Of course I said yes when the Director asked if Natalie could stay with me. She felt that we would have some things in common. But the timing couldn't be worse." Rosie squeezed her eyes shut. "Planning the Independence Day festivities is exhausting. And Natalie is a full-time project. The cook is keeping an eye on her today, but she is my responsibility."

Carter let out a snort. "No offense, Rosie, but there's no way this little princess should be causing you so much stress. How bad can she be? She's just a kid!"

Rosie opened one weary brown eye.

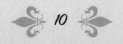

"Carter, you have no idea. She's a—a nightmare."

Carter knew that with all the pressure Rosie was under, taking care of Natalie could become the straw that breaks the camel's back. And she couldn't let that happen.

"What if I watch Natalie tomorrow?" Carter suggested. "That way, you can do whatever you need to do to get ready for the celebration."

Rosie sat up. "Really, Carter? You wouldn't mind?"

"No prob," Carter said, shrugging. It would give her something to do while Rosie was busy. And while she had disliked having to show Rosie around her school at first, it had ended up being kind of fun teaching a princess how to be a regular teenager. Teaching a princess how to be a real *kid* would be even easier.

"Carter, you are the best friend ever," Rosie said, a huge smile on her face. "If anyone can make Natalie listen, it is you!"

A commotion at the opposite end of the pool made the two friends look up. Waiters were scurrying out of the way as a young girl ran past them, wildly waving a large green pool noodle and chasing Gracie, a Cavalier King Charles spaniel that belonged to the palace cook.

"*Returnez*, you scoundrel!" Natalie shouted, wielding the noodle like a sword. "I will slice you! I will dice you!"

"So that's Natalie, huh?" Carter asked. She was beginning to wonder what she'd just gotten herself into.

Rosie gave Carter a *see-what-I-mean* look, but Carter just folded her arms and smirked. "I think I have my work cut out for me," she said confidently.

Chapter 2

"How did you sleep?" Rosie asked Carter the next morning as they walked down a palace corridor. The queen wore a flowered sundress, her long hair pulled back on one side with a red barrette. Carter had opted for her usual summer attire—tank top, cargo shorts, and a pair of sneakers.

Sunlight splashed through tall windows onto the floral-patterned carpet, and the air smelled of fresh flowers.

"Like a princess," Carter told her, smiling politely at a palace maid who walked briskly down the hallway with a feather duster. They'd spent the rest of yesterday afternoon hanging out by the pool and catching up. Rosie seemed to relax more and more as they lounged and chatted. Carter had been happy to see her friend taking a well-deserved break.

"Me, too," Rosie said gratefully. "Carter, I can't thank you enough for watching Natalie. Knowing you will be with her puts my mind at ease. Here we are," she said, as they arrived at a closed door. She gave a light knock, then pushed the door open.

The spacious guest room had a beautiful view of the palace grounds and was decorated in bright bold colors.

It was also one of the messiest bedrooms Carter had ever seen. Clothes were tossed everywhere. Shoes spilled out of two large trunks. Tiny game cartridges that Carter knew cost a lot of money were scattered on the floor, right next to an iPod that was just waiting to be stepped on. Three huge

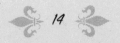

shopping bags of toys sat by the window, still unopened.

"Bonjour, Natalie," Rosie said cheerfully. "I wanted to introduce you to my good friend Carter. She's going to be visiting with us for a few days."

Natalie lay on top of a four-post king-size bed. She wore a pair of lavender satin pajamas and was busy clicking a TV remote. A furry sleep mask depicting a monkey wearing a tiara was pushed up on her head like a headband.

"Hey, Natalie," Carter said, giving a little wave.

Natalie didn't look at her. She was focused intently on flipping the channels.

"See what I mean?" Rosie whispered. She walked across the room and pushed aside the curtains, letting sunlight fill the room. "It's a beautiful day, Natalie. Time to get up and get dressed. You're going to spend some time with Carter today."

"Because you're too busy," Natalie said flatly.

Carter shook her head. "Because *I* know how to have fun and I heard you like to have fun, too."

"I need to eat first," Natalie said.

"Looks like you have quite a selection to choose from," Carter said, frowning over at a stack of dish-laden trays on the floor.

"Pancakes with strawberries are gross," Natalie said, pointing to the first tray. "I only like Lucky Charms without milk," she said with a nod to the second tray. Then she picked up a banana that lay next to her on the bed. "And this banana has a brown spot on it, so I can't eat it." She collapsed back on the pillows, as if all the explanations were too much for her.

Just then, there was a rap on the door. It was a servant named Marie, carrying a small tray with toast and a glass of milk.

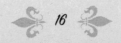

"Is there jam on that toast?" Natalie said, wrinkling her nose. "I smell jam."

Marie glanced nervously at Rosie.

Rosie swiftly stepped in and took the tray. "Thank you, Marie. Please tell the cook that will be all for today." She placed the tray on the nightstand. "Now Natalie, I know your parents would not be happy with that behavior."

"They're not happy *ever*," Natalie mumbled. She pressed the remote's volume button and the TV got louder and louder.

"I'm sorry, Carter. I've got to go," Rosie said, apologizing, as she glanced down at her diamond-encrusted watch. "It's time for my first meeting." She raised her voice to be heard over the TV. "I hate to leave you like this, but—"

"Don't worry about me," Carter said, walking over to the TV and turning it off. "Worry about her."

After Rosie scooted out the door, Carter stared down at the pint-size princess. "Okay, Natalie. Look, I know you're a princess. Rosie told me everything."

"And did she tell you it's a secret?" Natalie asked.

"Yep." Carter picked up a piece of toast and took a loud, noisy bite. "I'm good with secrets."

She dropped her canvas tote bag and sat down hard on the bed, bouncing a surprised Natalie. "See, I'm away from home this week, too. Rosie's kind of busy, and it looks like I'm going to have a lot of free time. So she thought it might be fun for us to hang out together."

Natalie gave her a suspicious look. "Hang out?" she asked. "You mean like friends?"

Carter nodded. "And Rosie thought that maybe I could teach you a little bit about blending in with other people. Help keep your identity a secret while you're here."

The princess considered this. "So are you like some kind of tutor?"

"Um, yeah. I guess you could call it that." Carter took the pillow from underneath Natalie's head and gave it a firm plumping. "Now, in the morning, kids get dressed, make their beds, and eat their breakfast—which, by the way, normally doesn't come on a silver tray." She handed Natalie the plate with the remaining piece of toast.

Natalie's mouth scrunched into an unhappy pout. "Do I have to eat this?"

Carter nodded again. "Because regular kids listen to people who are older and bigger than they are."

As Natalie took a tiny bite of her toast, Carter surveyed the room, hands on her hips. "Now. Unless you want Rosie's staff to

think you're a total slob, it's time to exchange that tiara for a vacuum."

"That was totally boring," Natalie said as she folded the last remaining T-shirt and put it in a drawer. "I don't want to do it again."

Carter shrugged. "Then don't let it get so bad again. Picking up your stuff is twice as boring the second time you have to do it."

"That's what maids are for, Carter," Natalie said in a singsong voice. "Did you know I have three of them who work just for me?"

"I hope they get paid a lot of cold, hard cash," Carter muttered under her breath. Surprisingly, it had only taken a half hour to get things tidied up. Now it was time for Carter to get started on the plan she'd thought up while they were working.

If I am going to spend the entire day

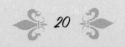

with this kid, we have got to get out of the palace, she thought.

Carter knew just where to take Natalie. She'd learned all about a downtown farmer's market from several palace staffers. The people, the cool food, the local color—it sounded like a lot of fun.

She walked over to where the little princess was standing, looking at her reflection in a large oval mirror. The girl's legs looked pale in her white shorts. Her yellow T-shirt with a horse on it and fuchsia flip-flops with faux pink and green jewels reminded Carter just how old Natalie was. And she's probably scared, too, Carter thought.

"Listen, I've got an idea," she said. "Palaces can be kind of stuffy, and Rosie told me that you haven't left the grounds since you arrived."

Natalie frowned. "*Oui*. I've been a prisoner."

"What do you say we break out of here?" Carter asked, walking over to the bedroom door and opening it. She made a big show of looking up and down the hall. "Looks like the coast is clear," she stage-whispered. "Grab your sunglasses. We'll make a run for it."

Natalie pulled on a yellow baseball cap and darted over to the door. "Did you bring any weapons?" she whispered back, unexpectedly playing along.

"Just my sparkling wit and personality," Carter said, stepping into the hall and leading the way toward the stairs.

Please, she thought as they crept down the deserted corridor, let that be enough.

"So, where is it we're going?" Natalie asked as they bumped down a grassy knoll. "It is so hot here," she complained, wiping a hand across her perfectly dry forehead. They had caught a ride on one of the palace golf carts—that was how everyone at the palace got around—and now they were riding across the manicured grounds toward the main road that lay just outside the palace gates.

"The farmer's market," Carter explained for the fourth time. "It's an outdoor market that's held twice a week in Pamalisah, the largest city in Costa Luna. There are vendors from all over the country, and the food is supposed to be incredible. And there are music and street magicians." It was definitely worth spending an afternoon there.

Natalie sighed. "It will have to be better than another day at the palace. The food is terrible here, Carter. No *pain au chocolat*, no mint-chocolate-chip gelato—I could not *believe* it when that cook gave me the news."

"And they even put milk in your Lucky Charms!" Carter said in mock indignation.

The sarcasm was lost on Natalie. "I

know. Terrible! And do you know that they only get twenty-five channels on TV here? I have never even heard of such a thing."

Carter opened her mouth and then shut it. Instead, she exchanged a glance with the golf-cart driver, Mr. David. He looked like he was trying not to laugh.

That's the best way to handle this, Carter decided—laugh Natalie's crankiness off. And maybe, just maybe, she'd be able to talk some common sense into that little tiaraless head.

Mr. David pulled to a stop in front of the gate. "Here you are, ladies. Enjoy your day. And please, Carter, call us if you need anything at all." He motioned to the security guards manning the palace gates, and slowly they started to swing open.

"Thanks," Carter called as they hopped out of the golf cart and walked through the palace's main entrance. The gate shut quietly behind them, leaving them on a white concrete sidewalk lined by palm trees that curved around the bend in the road.

"It's good manners to thank someone when they help you," she told Natalie.

"But you thanked him," Natalie replied. "That covered both of us."

Carter raised an eyebrow, then began to walk.

"What are we doing?" Natalie asked, jogging to catch up. A few mopeds sped by them, and an occasional car. Her eyes narrowed. "You don't actually expect me to walk to town, do you?"

Carter let out a snort. "Of course not," she replied calmly. She pulled out her cell phone to check the time, then put her hand up to her eyes, shielding them from the sunlight. "Should be any second now," she said, coming to a stop by a cement bench. She rocked back and forth on the balls of her feet, squinting into the distance. "Yep. There it is."

She couldn't resist a tiny laugh at the look on Natalie's pinched face. They weren't going to walk all the way to Pamalisah. That would have been too hot and sweaty, even for Carter.

Nope. They were going to ride there—only not in a limousine the way Natalie was used to.

Carter held up her hand to signal a city bus crowded with local residents on their way to work. The windows were rolled down—clearly, there wasn't any air-conditioning—and by the look of things, there weren't any available seats, either.

"Welcome to public transportation," Carter said, taking the stunned princess's hand and pulling her up the bus steps.

Chapter 3

*A*fter only three minutes on a crowded bus with Her Royal Highness Natalie de Rouen, Carter wondered if taking her out of the palace had been a good idea after all. There wasn't anything that the little princess didn't complain about. A-n-y-t-h-i-n-g.

Too hot? Check.

Too crowded? Check.

Too bumpy? Check.

Too *friendly*? Check, check, check.

"I like your shirt," a little girl a few years younger than Natalie said quietly. Then she ducked under her mother's arm.

"Thank you," Natalie said primly. She

turned her head, then whispered to Carter, "I'm not supposed to talk to people I don't know. Make her go away."

Carter rolled her eyes. "She does look pretty dangerous," she whispered back while smiling over at the little girl. "They always say watch out for first graders in sundresses. Especially the ones with pigtails."

As Natalie sulkily crossed her arms, Carter gazed out the open window. The Costa Luna countryside was truly beautiful—low hills dotted with villas, and rugged cliffs jutting out into impossibly blue water. In the distance, Carter could see tiny islands covered with lush vegetation. Catamarans and fishing boats bobbed in the water.

And Rosie is in charge of it all, Carter marveled, feeling really proud of her friend.

Carter knew how lucky she was to be Rosie's friend—and to get the chance to visit her country. Even if she did have to stand for ten minutes on a hot bus babysitting a princess. Luckily they'd finally gotten seats.

"Besides," Natalie went on, "that girl made me feel sad."

"Why?" Carter asked.

"What she said. It reminded me of Shimmer."

"Shimmer?" Carter prompted.

Natalie pointed to the horse on her shirt. "*Mon cheval*. My pony. Father promised he'd give him the sweetest, grassiest hay, and Mother said she'd make sure Shimmer had all the sugar cubes and raisins he wants, even if the servants have to make a trip to the store in the middle of the night."

Why am I not surprised? Carter thought, shaking her head. Of course Natalie had a pony named Shimmer. And probably a cat named Fuffy, a dog named Rover, and a rabbit, a goldfish, and a gerbil, too. All of which were no doubt taken care of by servants.

The bus rounded a corner, revealing the vivid aqua ocean. Carter pulled out her camera and snapped a few pictures. "Have you ever seen anything so gorgeous?" she asked. She looked back to Natalie, who could only shrug. Of course she had.

But there was a good chance—no, a great chance—that even though Natalie had probably been exposed to some of the most exciting places in the world, she'd never gotten the chance to experience them as a normal girl would.

Carter was determined to change that.

"Wow," she said, mustering up all the enthusiasm she could when they pulled into the heart of Pamalisah a few minutes later. "Can you believe it? We're here already!" The bus pulled up to its main city stop in front of a row of benches.

"It took long enough," Natalie said with a pout. "We could have walked faster than this garbage can on wheels got us here!"

Carter took her hand, and with a quick "thank you" to the driver, climbed off the bus. Trying to stay calm, she gazed around and collected her thoughts. Remember, she's only nine, Carter told herself. Remember, she must miss her parents. Remember, she's not used to being a regular kid. And the most important thing: if I don't bring her back to the palace in one piece, Rosie will kill me.

"Okay," Carter said, clapping her hands. The faint sound of music rippled in the breeze. "Who's ready to have some fun?"

"Why couldn't we stay back at the palace?" Natalie whined, dragging her feet as they walked down a cobblestone sidewalk. "This is so boring!"

"Maybe if you started checking out all the cool stuff they have here, you'd have a better time." I know I would, Carter thought, exasperated. In the forty minutes they'd been in Pamalisah, they'd visited some of the little shops in town, and now they were approaching the open-air farmer's market.

"And you have to stop talking about the palace," Carter reminded her in a low whisper. "Remember, you need to blend in like a regular girl. It's important, Natalie."

"It's not easy to pretend you're not special when you are," Natalie said. Carter held in a groan and kept walking.

The market was filled with colorful stalls, where local farmers sold fresh fruits and vegetables, cheeses, and flowers. Vendors displayed jewelry and scarves and items made from native materials.

"So what would you like to do first?" Carter asked. "We could get some lemonade and churros. Or maybe check out those beaded belts over there?"

Natalie tilted her chin toward a face-painting stall. "I want to get my face painted."

"Okay," Carter said, glad that the princess had at last found something she liked. They walked over to the stall as a boy with a gecko painted on his face happily skipped away with his father.

"Hello," said a woman sitting on a stool. Next to her was a table filled with tiny pots of paint and several brushes. "What would you like? A tiger? A peacock? Maybe some hearts?"

"A butterfly," Natalie said, pointing to a laminated chart that showed several different designs. "Just like that."

The woman smiled. "You'll be the prettiest butterfly ever."

Natalie sat down on the stool, and the woman expertly began to paint the outline of butterfly wings on her cheeks.

"Are you done yet?" Natalie asked after just a few minutes.

"Shhh," Carter said. "Don't fidget. You've got to let the paint dry."

"That's right," the woman said, selecting another brush. She was coloring in the wings. "Otherwise, the colors blend and you need to start over again."

"You're really good," Carter said as she watched the woman work. She was almost tempted to get her own face painted.

The woman smiled. "Plenty of practice." She added some glitter as a finishing touch and then held up a mirror to Natalie. "*Bonita.* Beautiful."

Natalie frowned, wrinkling her purple-painted nose. "It doesn't look like the picture."

Carter looked at the chart then back at Natalie. "Yes it does."

"No it doesn't!" Natalie stood up and stomped her foot. "The one in the picture is purple and magenta. Mine is purple and pink!"

The woman looked uncertainly at

Carter. "I am sorry. I didn't have magenta. I didn't think—"

"It's totally fine. We love it." Carter hurriedly handed her some money. "Thank you so much."

"You shouldn't have paid her," Natalie said as Carter quickly walked her away. "I told her what I wanted, and she didn't give it to me. She didn't deserve to be rewarded."

Carter stepped to the side so that people could pass by. She knelt down beside Natalie and looked her straight in the eye. "Getting paid for doing your job isn't a reward, Natalie. So it's pink, not magenta. Who cares?"

"*I* care. I expect things to be done the way they're supposed to be," Natalie told her. "Someone like you, with low standards, wouldn't understand."

Carter squeezed her eyes shut and used her dad's old trick. She counted to ten in her head and took a deep, calming breath. "Okay!"

She opened her eyes. "Time for lunch."

The market was really crowded now. They shuffled slowly along the rows of food vendors. "Yum," Carter said as they passed by a *churrascaría*. Her mouth watered when she saw the slow-turned beef and the huge bowls filled with pasta and corn salads. "How does that look?"

Natalie shook her head. "Too spicy."

"Mmm. Okay." They walked further into the market, dodging businessmen and women, and mothers pushing strollers. They passed a Middle Eastern–style food counter. Italian. Chinese. And Natalie had a reason why she couldn't eat at any of them.

"Let's look for a place that has French toast," Natalie said decisively after passing up at least ten places.

Breakfast? Now? Carter blew out her breath. "Let's not."

The princess stuck out her chin. "Then

let's go back to the first place. I'll try the beef. Maybe."

Carter stopped in her tracks. They were standing in front of a gumbo café, and suddenly all she wanted was a little taste of home. "We're eating here," she declared, pointing up to the large menu on the wall. "Have you ever had a po'boy?"

"Why would I ever have a poor any-thing?" Natalie said indignantly. "I am a rich girl. Get me French toast!"

That was it. That was really it. Carter strode over to the counter. "Two fresh cat-fish po'boys, one order of hush puppies, and two lemonades."

When the order was ready, she picked up one tray and handed it to Natalie. Or tried to. The little princess looked at the tray as if it were covered with worms.

"You expect me to carry your food? Like a servant?"

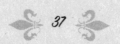

"It's *our* food," Carter said through gritted teeth. "And since I'm not *your* servant, we're going to work together."

With stiff outstretched arms, Natalie carried her tray and followed Carter to an open-air food court. They found a couple of seats in the center of the crowd and sat down.

Carter was starving, and the po'boy smelled delicious. She was already halfway through her sandwich when she noticed that Natalie had barely touched her food. Instead, she was glaring at Carter.

"Don't you know anything? You're supposed to wait for me to eat first."

Carter gaped at her. "Huh?"

Natalie pursed her lips. "I'm a princess," she said, drawing out each syllable. "I'm roy-al-ty. That means *I* go first all the time." She smoothed a paper napkin on her lap. "You don't know anything."

Carter put down her sandwich and leaned forward, her blood boiling. "I know that you are not being *polite*."

"I'm just telling you how I feel," Natalie said lightly. "It's not your fault you're dumb. I suppose only someone with royal blood would understand."

"Yeah? Well, I didn't want to say anything, but guess what? I'm a royal, too," Carter snapped. She sat back in her chair, a satisfied smirk on her face as she watched Natalie's mouth drop into an *O*. "So there."

Seeing the look of shock on Natalie's face was totally worth the outrageous lie she'd just told. Anybody in her situation would have done the same thing. For the first time that day, Natalie was speechless.

A trickle of sweat slid down the back of Carter's neck. She started to feel that maybe, just maybe, she'd made a big mistake. She'd just told a whopper of a lie. And stooping to the level of a bratty nine-year-old was not something to be proud of. She picked up her cup and took a big gulp of icy lemonade.

Humiliating as it was, she was going to have to tell Natalie the truth.

"Natalie, listen," Carter began, swallowing her pride. "I—" And she stopped talking.

She was too busy staring at the cutest guy she'd ever seen in her life. He was standing over by one of the vendor's stalls.

And he was looking straight back at her.

When a cute boy smiled at you there was only one thing to do. Hope you didn't have lettuce stuck in your teeth and wave him over.

"Did you save any for me?" he asked, walking over to their table, his eyes twinkling.

Natalie was still staring at Carter, flabbergasted. She barely even noticed the boy standing beside their table.

"Oh, too bad. If we'd known you were coming . . ." Carter said, trailing off. He was even cuter up close—tall with short, curly brown hair, brown eyes, and a friendly smile. He had on a pale blue shirt with the sleeves pushed up, baggy shorts, and a thin brown leather cord around his wrist.

"Andy," he said, extending his hand.

"Carter," she said, shaking it. The boys Carter knew back home definitely didn't shake hands with you. It was pretty adorable.

Natalie cleared her throat. "Oh. And that's Natalie," Carter said, giving the princess a *don't-blow-this* look. "We're, uh, visiting. I'm, um, a friend of her, uh, family."

"Nice face paint," Andy said, admiring the artist's handiwork on Natalie's face. "There's a butterfly sanctuary in the north of Costa Luna. You should go there if you have time."

"It's really beautiful here," Carter told him, feeling her heart race just a little faster. "You're lucky to live in such a pretty place."

Andy nodded. "It's cool. And you should see it on Independence Day. The place is crazy." He smiled. "I guess it's what it's like in your country on the Fourth of July. You're American, right?"

"Yeah," Carter said. "How did you know?"

Andy laughed. "No offense or anything, but you have 'tourist' written all over you."

Carter felt a blush creeping into her cheeks. She laughed it off as best she could before Andy noticed. "Well, it's so beautiful I have to take it all in while I'm here."

"How long will—"

"Guess what?" Natalie piped up then. She smiled wide as she looked at Andy. Natalie's voice dropped to a squeaky excited whisper as she continued, "Carter's not a regular person. She's royalty!"

Carter was horrified. What had started out as a silly, stupid lie was now a full-fledged, embarrassing nightmare. "Natalie—"

"But are you a princess?" Natalie demanded, looking at Carter. "A duchess? Or just a lady?"

Carter gulped. She was totally stuck. Andy was looking at her expectantly, waiting to hear her answer, too. She looked down at her sandal and gave a kind of half shrug. "Something like that," she mumbled, her cheeks flushing. When she looked back up, Andy was smiling at her. She realized then that it was definitely too late to tell him the truth. In the few short minutes they had been talking, Carter had felt an instant connection.

If she told him right then that she had just made up a ridiculous lie about being a member of a royal family, she'd look like the biggest idiot on the planet. Not to mention certifiable.

"That's really, uh, cool," Andy said. "So where—"

"I, uh, kind of want to keep it a secret," Carter interrupted. She flashed a sheepish grin.

"Oh, okay. No problem," Andy said. He gave her a reassuring smile, and Carter was filled with relief. She promised herself that if she met him again *alone* she would tell him the whole truth first thing.

They talked for a few more minutes and Carter discovered that Andy was just as nice as he was cute. She found out that he was a junior in high school here in Costa Luna. He was an avid baseball fan and followed the Boston Red Sox; his favorite food was a cheeseburger topped with fried onions; and his favorite color was green.

"So what would you have been doing now if you weren't talking to me?" Carter asked, tucking a stray piece of hair behind her ear.

A weird look crossed his face, and for a

second Carter wondered if maybe he had a girlfriend.

He looked forlornly down at the empty food wrappers on the table. "Eating," he said sadly.

For a moment she thought he was being serious. Then they both started laughing. "Do you want to get some ice cream or something?" he asked.

"Sounds good," Carter said, turning to Natalie. Or, more accurately, Natalie's empty chair.

Because the little princess was gone.

Chapter 4

"Natalie! Natalie, this isn't funny!" Carter called as she and Andy raced up and down the market's crowded aisles. Hard, cold panic had set in. How am I going to explain this to Rosie? Carter thought. I'm supposed to be teaching the princess how to be a regular person—not a *missing* person!

"Don't worry, Carter," Andy said, squeezing her hand. "Costa Luna is a small place. We'll find her."

Carter wanted to believe that was true. If I hadn't been so busy flirting with Andy, this never would have happened, she thought, as guilt coursed through her veins.

Now the cutest boy she'd met in a long time was holding her hand, and she couldn't even enjoy it. Instead, she felt like she was going to hurl.

Andy suggested they split up. "We'll have better odds that way." Fighting back panic, Carter took one aisle while Andy sprinted down another.

Carter walked quickly, swiveling her head. Was this some sort of stupid game? Was Natalie hiding underneath a table or behind a curtain, ready to pop out at her? Or had some lunatic kidnapped her?

Maybe she should call the P.P.P. The first few minutes after an abduction were critical, Carter knew. But she didn't know if the princess had been abducted. Carter was choking back a sob when she heard the most beautiful sound in the world. . . .

"That's unfair! You're upsetting me!"

Natalie's tiny, shrill voice carried over

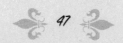

the market stalls. Carter ran toward the sound.

The princess was standing in front of a stall with several tables displaying handmade rings, bracelets, and earrings. Around her neck was a beautiful choker of smoky gray beads. The vendor, a middle-aged man, was glaring at her.

"He expects me to pay for it. Like, with money!" Natalie fumed to Carter as she rushed over. "Doesn't he understand that it is an honor for me to choose to wear his design? If someone takes a picture of me wearing this necklace, he'll make a lot of money. Everyone will want a necklace just like mine!"

Carter realized that even though this mission didn't involve international espionage, it was just as dire. She had to get this girl back to the palace ASAP to help her learn how to blend in—and to get her some manners.

"Take it off *now*," Carter hissed. Natalie actually listened to her. She meekly put the necklace back on the table and turned her back to it just as Andy came jogging up to them. His face lit up when he saw that Natalie was okay.

"I don't want that stupid necklace anyway," Natalie said, her eyes welling up with big, fat tears. "Everyone here is mean. I just want to go home."

"It was really nice meeting you," Carter told Andy, wishing more than anything that they could hang out some more. "But I think it's time Cinderella left the ball. She's about to turn into a pumpkin."

Andy pulled out his cell phone from his pocket. "Can I call you?"

Her pulse racing, Carter took the phone and punched in her cell phone number. "Sure. Cool." Fighting the urge to jump up and down, she gave him what she hoped was a nonchalant wave. Then she took Natalie by the arm and headed in the direction of the bus stop, smiling all the way.

Babysitting a princess had turned out to be a pretty good way to spend the afternoon after all.

"The menu is of utmost importance," Rosie's mother, Sophia, said as they walked over to a table on which several large warming dishes sat.

Their close friend and royal dress designer, Mr. Elegante, agreed. "You can have the loveliest decorations, entertainment, staff . . . but"—he held his nose—"if the food is no good, your party is a bomb."

Rosie gave a worried nod. That was why she had scheduled a menu preview today at the palace. Everything that was on the menu for the royal ball had been prepared for her and a small group of palace staffers and members of the press to sample.

There was tuna tartare in sesame-miso cones, Kobe-beef sliders, chicken *taquitos*, macaroni with four cheeses, fennel-and-pear salad, fresh-fruit kabobs, lobster, and caviar. . . .

The palace cook came out in his white chef's coat and hat. "This ball will kick off the Independence Day festivities and set the tone for the week ahead," he explained. "We are using as many local ingredients as we can—fish from the waters off Costa Luna, locally grown fruits and organic vegetables, wines from our vineyards. Your guests, Queen Rosalinda, are in for a culinary experience unlike any they've ever had."

And from the looks on everyone's faces as they sampled the food, it was going to be a yummy evening.

Mr. Elegante picked up a chocolate crown and broke off a piece. "Delicious."

Rosie nibbled on a *taquito*, but she wasn't really hungry. She was too busy running all the details over and over in her head. She wanted the royal ball to be absolutely perfect. Knowing that the food was great was only the first tiny step. There was still so much to do.

She felt her cell vibrate in her skirt pocket. When she saw the text message, she smiled. It was nice to get an urgent message from someone other than a caterer, a decorator, or a party-planner.

Her brown eyes widened in happy surprise as she read what Carter had to say.

```
baitgirl: rosie, omg, jst met
cutest boy ever!!!!!!!!!!!
```

Chapter 5

"You take the bread like this." Carter slapped two pieces of white bread onto a butcher-block countertop. "Then you open the jar and dip your knife into the peanut butter." She demonstrated, feeling like a TV chef. "Next, the jelly."

"You use the same knife for the jelly?" Natalie asked, her blue eyes wide with horror. They were in the massive palace kitchen, and Carter was doing her best to show the princess that not all meals arrived on silver platters.

Rosie was sitting at the large staff dining table with two assistants from the master-of-the-household department. They were in the midst of narrowing down place settings for the ball. Rosie was twirling her hair around her pencil and appeared to be deep in thought as the assistants talked about dinner plates and glasses.

"Yep. And don't even think about asking me to cut off the crusts." Carter smoothed down the jelly, put the sandwich together, and took a big bite. She licked some peanut butter from her lip. "Now your turn."

Natalie dutifully picked up the knife and repeated what Carter had done. "I don't see what this has to do with blending in," she grumbled. "Do you make your own food like this all the time?"

Carter swallowed past the lump in her throat as she thought back to the lie she'd told about being royal. "It has everything to do with blending," she said. "You—I mean, um, we, can't always expect people to do things for, uh, us. What if you want a snack and you're by yourself?"

"There's always a servant." Natalie finished making her sandwich and took a reluctant bite.

When they were finished with their snack and had cleaned up, they helped Rosie narrow down the four remaining place-setting choices to two. Then Carter reached into her pocket, pulled out a wad of American bills, and laid them out one by one on the white marble countertop.

"This is money," she told Natalie, explaining the obvious, which wasn't necessarily so obvious for a princess. "Normal people use it to pay for things." Carter nodded toward the bills. "Sometimes this, um, girl, works for my dad. Guess how much she gets paid for one hour?"

Natalie shrugged. "Fifty dollars?"

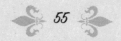

Carter snorted. "In my—I mean *her*—dreams." She reached over and slid a five-dollar bill and two ones across the counter. "Seven bucks. Now, do you know how much that necklace cost that you wanted today? In American money?"

"Seven dollars?" Natalie guessed.

Carter shook her head. "Twenty. If you earned seven dollars an hour, you'd have to work three hours to pay for that necklace."

Natalie definitely was paying close attention. Her brow creased as she exclaimed, "That necklace was not worth it! And your father should pay that girl more!"

Carter smiled. Her pupil was learning already.

Just as she was about to explain the fine art of tipping, Carter's phone vibrated. Her dad had texted her a little while ago asking where they kept the chili powder—he was actually cooking. Hmmm, what is it now . . . paprika? Carter thought, opening her phone.

But it wasn't her dad.

bsbllfn57: hey how r u?

"Yes!" Carter gave a victory arm pump and Rosie glanced over, raising a questioning eyebrow.

"Tell you later," Carter mouthed. Other than a few quick texts, Carter hadn't had a moment alone with Rosie to dish about her afternoon. She thought for a moment, then texted back.

baitgirl: good! u?

bsbllfn57: tired. m glad i met u 2day.

baitgirl: ya me 2

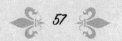

bsbllfn57: what's going on?

baitgirl: helpin nat with a
project

Natalie grabbed Carter's phone. "Can I say something?" And before Carter knew what was happening, Natalie typed:

baitgirl: u r relly cute

Carter shrieked and chased the princess around the kitchen island. "What do you think you're doing?"

"It's from that boy at the market, isn't it?" Natalie asked, a gleam in her eye. "I can tell. You have that mushy-gushy look."

Carter was sure she didn't have a mushy-gushy look. Well, maybe just a slight swoon.

Natalie faced her down across the island top. "If you like him, why don't you just tell him?"

"Who said I like him?" Carter asked coolly.
Natalie giggled and hit SEND. "You did."

Carter cringed. Spending the day with Natalie had been slightly painful. But waiting to see if Andy would respond to that last text would be absolute torture.

Later that night, Carter was giddy with excitement as she planned her date with Andy for the next day.

bsbllfn57: wht tm do u wnt 2 mt?

baitgirl: hmmm myb 9

bsbllfn57: cool. where?

baitgirl: um hw abt the light-house?

Bsbllfn57: sounds gd-l8r

It was almost ten p.m. Carter had gone to her room and changed into a supersoft T-shirt and flannel boxers. She had spent the past half hour texting with Andy. Rosie had moved on to selecting table linens and was in deep discussion with her staff, while Natalie was under the watch of Henri, one of the palace servants.

Poor Henri, Carter thought, wondering what Natalie had the older man doing. A five-thousand-piece puzzle? A duel with pool noodles? Hide-and-seek across the palace grounds?

She snuggled into the pillows of her queen-size guest bed, thankful she wasn't responsible for planning a ball or babysitting right now. The only thing she had to do was flirt via text message.

Carter didn't know Andy that well, but he seemed really cool. And even cooler was the fact that *he'd* asked *her* if she wanted to hang out tomorrow. And he hadn't even mentioned Natalie's text!

Hmmm. Hang out with a hot guy or chase after a bossy pint-size princess? A total no-brainer.

She'd have to check with Rosie to make sure that spending the day with Andy was okay. She's probably got tons more things to do, Carter thought, a little sad that she wasn't spending more time with her friend. But I don't want her to feel guilty about leaving me alone, and if she knows that I'm off having fun, she'll be happier. That was just how Rosie was.

The lighthouse was the perfect place to meet Andy: neutral and very public. It had seemed weird to ask him to pick her up at the palace—that could open up the door to a lot of questions she definitely didn't feel like answering.

Rosie had pointed out the lighthouse on

Carter's first day in Costa Luna. Because it was one of the highest spots in the country, it was a big tourist attraction. And it was just a short walk from the palace gates.

Carter put her phone in her pocket and jumped out of bed. *I've got to go tell Rosie about my date,* she thought. She had to be done with the linens by now—how long could it take to pick out napkin colors?

Carter opened her bedroom door and padded barefoot down the quiet corridor. At night there was a different vibe to the palace. The royal household's daytime staff had either gone home or retired to their quarters, and the nighttime staff on duty was much smaller.

When she reached the kitchen, Carter popped her head inside. Empty. She was standing there, hesitating, when a palace servant rounded the corner.

"If you are looking for Queen Rosalinda,

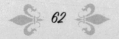

she is meeting with Lord Chamberlain," he said politely. "They are in the queen's office going over the security for the parade route."

"Oh," Carter said, deflated. "Thanks." There was no way she could interrupt Rosie now. *Hi, I know you guys are probably talking about top secret security issues, but can I just tell Rosie about the cute guy I met?*

Carter looked around, trying to decide what to do. She could go for a swim, but she didn't really like swimming by herself. *Maybe I can find a good book to read,* she thought, walking past the royal library. She tiptoed inside and turned on a lamp.

Huge wooden shelves went all the way to the fourteen-foot-high ceilings. They were filled with leather-bound books, their spines embossed with gold. On one wall hung framed drawings and maps, and a huge globe sat on a stand in the corner. Two velvet couches faced each other in front of a fire-place.

Somehow, I don't think they're going to have something light and romantic, Carter said to herself, as she pulled a book off a shelf—*The History of Costa Lunan Reptiles and Amphibians: 18th Century*—and quickly put it back.

Feeling kind of lonely, Carter walked back out of the room and stared down the corridor. At the far end she noticed an open door. Light spilled out onto the carpet. Curious, she walked toward it. It was hard to remember what all the rooms were used for, but this one, Carter recalled, was the palace's version of a family room.

I wonder who's in there, she thought, approaching the door. Sophia? She glanced inside.

To her surprise, Natalie was sitting on a huge couch sipping some fruit punch through a straw. She looked just as lonely as Carter felt.

"Hey," Carter said, giving the little princess a wary smile. She was surprised to see her still up. "What's going on?"

Natalie shrugged. "Nothing."

"Are you all by yourself?" Carter asked, looking around the empty room.

Natalie shook her head. "Henri is with me. He went to get a bowl of popcorn. We are going to watch a movie."

"Oh, cool. What one?"

"*Fairy Butterfly Sparkles*," Natalie said, her face lighting up. "Have you seen it?"

"Can't say that I have," Carter told her. And she had a feeling Henri hadn't either. She was about to make some excuse about having to go wash her hair when Natalie surprised her.

"You can stay and watch it with us. If you want," she added.

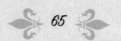

Aww, man, Carter thought as she paused in the doorway. She so didn't want to. But it wasn't like she had anything better to do. It would give Henri the out he most certainly wanted. And Rosie would appreciate it. "Um . . . okay," she said, joining the princess on the couch.

"I heard the movie is really, really good," Natalie said, picking up the remote. "And it's not even in theaters yet!"

"Then how can we watch it?" Carter asked her.

"Duh!" Natalie said. "The studio sent it over to Rosie special. Because she's royal." The little princess gave Carter a skeptical look. "That's what they do for *royals*."

Carter didn't miss a beat. "Yep, that's what they do." If she wasn't careful, her secret would be out of the bag.

But maybe it should be. That would be one less thing she'd need to worry about.

Before she could decide whether or not to tell Natalie the truth, Henri came back with some napkins and a huge ceramic bowl that said POPCORN. He bowed. "Hello, Miss Carter. I didn't know that you would be joining us. May I get you a drink?"

Carter smiled at him. "No, thanks, Henri. If you don't mind, me and Natalie thought we'd like to watch the movie—just the two of us."

"Really?" Henri asked, raising an eyebrow. "Are you sure?"

Carter nodded. "Unless you want to hang with us."

Henri handed the girls the popcorn bowl. "If you promise to tell me all about it, I am happy to leave the viewing to the two of you," he said. Then he practically ran out of the room.

Thirty minutes later, Carter was staring in amazement.

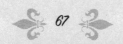

Because *Fairy Butterfly Sparkles* was one of the best movies she'd seen in years! Awesome costumes, a cute plot, funny dialogue . . . and she never would have watched it if it hadn't been for Natalie.

"Do you think the unicorn is going to find its way home?" Natalie whispered, biting her lip. She'd moved closer to Carter, her little blond head leaning against Carter's shoulder.

"Definitely," Carter whispered back, grabbing a handful of popcorn. "That sparkle fairy he met in the meadow is going to show him the way in the moonlight."

Natalie looked up at Carter. "I got lost once when we were visiting a museum. My mother was very upset. She even cried when they found me, but she said they were happy tears." Natalie seemed to be on the verge of crying herself. "I miss my mother, Carter," she said, her voice quiet. "Do you think I'll see her soon?"

Carter swallowed. She didn't want to give the kid false hope, but . . . "I hope so," she said. "I'm sure she misses you very much."

That seemed to satisfy Natalie. "Okay. And Carter?"

"Yes?"

Natalie handed over her now-empty punch bottle. "I need a refill."

"Really? You're not kidding?" Rosie asked.

Carter shook her head. "If you don't count that I had to get her two refills of punch, microwave more popcorn, and sing along with the theme song, I actually had a good time hanging with Her Majesty."

It was late—after midnight—and Rosie had stopped by Carter's room on her way to her private suite. The two girls were sprawled across the sateen duvet on Carter's bed, catching up.

Rosie rested her chin in her hands. "But

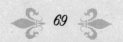

forget the movie. Let's talk boys. Specifically, cute Costa Luna boys named Andy."

Carter let out a dreamy sigh. "Yeah. Tall, dark, handsome . . . besides the tiny problem of him thinking I'm a royal, we're all good."

"Don't you think you better tell him the truth, Carter?" Rosie asked, looking serious.

Carter nibbled on a fingernail. "Do I have to?"

"Well, you don't *have* to. But I believe it is better to be honest, Carter."

"Oh, right. And aren't you the one who pretended to be plain old Rosie González, Your Highness?" Carter asked, even though she knew it was ridiculous to compare her current predicament to Rosie's earlier one.

Rosie started laughing. "That was a matter of my security, Carter. This is—"

"A matter of personal humiliation!" Carter rolled onto her back. "I will tell him," she vowed. Someday. Maybe when I'm back in Louisiana I can send him a text, she thought. Wimp.

"And I will keep Natalie here at the palace tomorrow. I do appreciate everything you did with her today."

"No prob," Carter said, shrugging. The bossy little princess had kind of grown on Carter—but she was glad she wouldn't have her tagging along on her date.

"I can't believe I have a real live date tomorrow," Carter said, nervous excitement whooshing through her. "Is there anything I should know about Costa Lunan boys?"

"Yes," Rosie said, a serious expression on her face. "They are my royal subjects. If Andy is anything other than a gentleman, it's straight to the dungeon for him."

Carter laughed. "That would be so cool if you could really do that."

Rosie dead-eyed her. "I can."

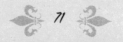

Chapter 6

"Isn't it great?" Andy asked, waving his arm like a game-show host over the breathtaking scenery in front of them.

"Yeah. And just think, it only took us nine hundred steps to climb up here," Carter told him, only half kidding. When she'd suggested meeting at the lighthouse, she didn't think they'd actually *climb* it. But Andy had insisted, saying it was the best view of Costa Luna you could find.

Stop thinking of it as a date, Carter cautioned herself. Think of it as hanging out with a new friend.

A new *cute* friend.

Andy held up the informational brochure they'd received when they entered the old lighthouse. "Two hundred fifty-five steps to be exact," he said. "But face it, where else do you get the chance to see migrating whales?"

Andy wasn't as cute as Carter had remembered him—he was cuter. Today he had on a pair of navy draw-cord shorts, a green T-shirt, and brown leather treads. His brown curls poked out from under a faded Red Sox baseball cap.

He had been right on time, which Carter liked. Keeping a girl waiting was not cool.

Neither is telling somebody you're a member of a royal family when you aren't, Carter thought for the zillionth time. To be fair, she hadn't technically told that whopper of a lie—Natalie was the guilty party. But I didn't do anything to correct it, she reminded herself. Instead, I went along with it.

Carter sighed inwardly. She would have to fess up to the truth. But until he brought it up . . . not yet.

She pulled out her camera and snapped a few pictures.

"Would you like one of you two together?" a woman wearing rhinestone sunglasses asked.

"Oh. Uh, sure," Carter said, handing the woman her camera. Wait. She had to try to sound at least a little royal. She cleared her throat. "I mean, yes. That's so very kind of you."

Andy gave her a funny look before they turned and smiled for the picture. Did he suspect she was lying? Her stomach churned nervously. She'd have to do a better job of acting like a princess.

"You look so familiar," the woman told Andy, tapping her chin with her finger. She gave Carter her camera. "Are you a student at Karate Kicks, by any chance?"

Andy shook his head and began to walk over to the stairwell. "Nope, not me."

"Thank you," Carter called out to the woman. She caught up with Andy. He seemed in a hurry to leave.

"I want to show you *my* Costa Luna," he told her as they began their descent down the creaky circular staircase. "The real one most tourists never see."

Carter took a careful step. Falling down the stairs would definitely not be royal. "That sounds . . . lovely."

If someone had told Carter three days ago that she'd be riding on the back of a sleek black Vespa scooter, her arms around a cute boy, her hair blowing in the Costa Lunan breeze, she'd have said they were crazy.

Well, maybe not the hair-blowing-in-the-breeze part. But the Vespa? And cute boy? That had definitely not been on her list of what to expect in Costa Luna.

"This is so fun!" she called out before she could stop to consider the way a royal would say it. She hoped Andy could hear her over the hum of the engine and the wind. Goose bumps had formed on her arms, and she was glad she'd decided to wear her red-and-white striped T-shirt instead of a tank top.

"I love to ride," he yelled back. "It's what I do when I need to think . . . get away from everything."

At first Carter had been a tiny bit nervous about getting on the Vespa. My dad would freak, she had thought nervously as she strapped on a helmet and driving glasses and listened carefully to Andy explain where to sit and how to hold on.

But once Andy had pulled out onto the road and they'd ridden for a few minutes, she'd started to relax. By the way Andy handled the Vespa, she could tell he was an experienced driver. And she could see the advantages of being on the scooter—not only could they zip in and out of traffic, they could park in the smallest of spaces.

Carter kept her arms firmly around Andy's waist and let her chin rest gently on his shoulder. He smelled like a mixture of shampoo and sunblock.

They were on a winding two-lane highway that, if you never strayed off of it, would eventually come full circle. Carter tried her best to take everything in: the brightly painted homes, the bougainvilleas spilling over cobbled fences, children flying kites on a school playground, birds flying in formation.

Andy turned off the main highway and slowed down as they left the asphalt road for a dirt one. They rode for a few minutes under a lush canopy of trees. Then, Andy pulled the Vespa to a stop under a shady willow.

"Are you okay? Having fun?" he asked, as

he climbed off and extended a hand to help Carter.

"Absolutely." Carter removed her helmet and shook out her hair. "Where are we?"

Andy motioned her toward a curving path. "Follow me."

Ahead of them was a large gnarled tree with a wooden sign that read Costa Luna Carvers. Huge clumps of what looked like tree roots tangled up in each other lined the path.

"Those are stumps," Andy said as they walked toward a large open-air woodshop. "This place is filled with some of the most talented wood-carvers in the world."

There were tons of tables filled with all sorts of things—jewelry boxes, mirrors, serving pieces—all made by hand. Scattered around the shop were pieces of wooden furniture in various stages of completion.

"What kind of wood is this?" Carter

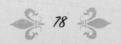

asked, picking up a beautiful bowl. "It's so pretty."

"Mahogany," Andy said. He waved to one of the carvers, who got up from his bench to greet them.

"Hey, Manny." Andy and the man shook hands. "This is my friend, Carter. She's visiting Costa Luna for a few days."

Manny smiled broadly. "Welcome to our shop, Carter."

"Thank you," Carter said. She ran her fingers over a sculpture. "Your stuff is so cool."

"We're very proud of our work here," Manny continued. "We craft our objects from native wood, and all our efforts are environmentally conscious."

Carter looked around as a butterfly fluttered past. It was the perfect place to get a souvenir for her dad. She and Andy browsed for a few minutes, and Carter decided on a beautiful glossy wood sculpture.

"And no visit to Costa Luna is complete without a commemorative magnet," Andy said, holding one up. It was a small wooden heart. "For you," he said, handing it to Carter as he paid for it. "Because I hope that Costa Luna will capture your heart."

"Why, it most certainly has," Carter replied in the most princessy voice possible.

When they pulled up to the dilapidated-looking shack, Carter tried to think positive. The place looked like a dump, but Andy promised that they had the best burgers and grilled fish sandwiches in Costa Luna.

"I bet you bring all the girls here," Carter joked as they walked up a rickety pair of steps and into the restaurant. Oops, she thought. That was a totally nonroyal thing to say! Royals didn't really joke about dating.

"Only those I'm trying to impress," Andy said, holding the door for her.

Without a doubt, Andy had been raised right. From helping her off the Vespa to holding open the door, his good manners definitely made him stand out. No Costa Lunan dungeon for him, she thought with a smile.

An old R&B song was playing on the radio, and most of the tables in the tiny place were filled. The smell of burgers grilling hung in the air, and Carter's stomach grumbled. I hope Andy didn't hear that, she thought, coughing loudly to cover up any further sounds. Suddenly, she was starving.

The grill guy gave Andy a friendly wave. "The regular, sir?" he called over, putting a couple buns on the grill.

Sir? So formal. Carter turned to Andy. "Do you know everyone in Costa Luna?"

Andy shrugged. "It's a small place. Hard not to."

Their food arrived a few minutes later,

and they snagged an empty table. Carter was halfway through her burger when she remembered that princesses didn't gobble up their food. When Rosie had tried a cheeseburger for the first time in Louisiana, she'd used actual *utensils*.

Carter clutched the burger in her fingers and thought for a moment. She could put the burger down on her plate and ask for a knife and fork. . . .

"What?" Andy asked, giving her a puzzled look. He had a dollop of ketchup on his chin.

Carter giggled. And that was it. He looked so sweet, and trying to pretend she was a royal was impossible. She couldn't be oh-so-very-proper.

I just have to be me, she thought.

"It's just . . . well," Carter stammered, trying to think of the right words to say. *I let you think I was royal because I like you and*

I felt embarrassed that I'd lied to Natalie.

She couldn't do it, she realized.

Not when she had half of a burger to finish and a long scooter ride back to the palace. Plus, she was having one of the best afternoons of her entire life.

"There's, um, some ketchup on your chin." She reached over and dabbed it off with her napkin.

"What if I wanted it there?" Andy said with a mischievous grin.

Carter glanced over at the ketchup bottle on the table. "We can arrange that."

It was that gorgeous time of day when the sun was just starting its slow creep downward. Carter and Andy pulled up at the palace gates, and Andy cut the engine. After lunch, they'd finished their tour of Costa Luna, stopping at a small beach that had the most amazing seashells and a park where

Andy showed Carter a rabbit burrow in the ground, hidden from view with twigs and pieces of fluff.

It had been a great day. And now it was over.

"So this is where you're staying, huh?" Andy asked, looking through the gates at the palace. "You never told me exactly—"

"Yes, home sweet home," Carter interrupted, not wanting to dig an even deeper hole for herself. "And I'd, um, invite you inside, but . . ." Carter trailed off, suddenly uncomfortable. She hadn't been able to come up with an alternative to the palace when he asked where she was staying. At least I told the truth about something, she thought, the guilt washing over her.

She slid off the Vespa and handed her helmet and safety glasses to Andy.

"No sweat. I'm totally not dressed for it," he joked, looking down at his wrinkled shorts and leather sandals. "I had a great time with you today."

"Me, too," Carter said, feeling kind of shy. She shuffled her feet, not sure what to say or do.

"So, how much longer are you here for?" he asked.

"Three more days," Carter told him.

"Wow."

Carter wasn't sure how she was supposed to interpret that. Was it like, *Wow, you're going home so soon?* Or, *Wow, you have a lot of time left?* Or, *Wow, I think I'm going to kiss you?*

It was the third kind of wow.

Andy gave her a quick kiss on the lips, then looked quickly around as if to make sure no one had spotted them.

"I'd better go. I'll call you," he said, hopping on the Vespa.

"Okay. Yeah," Carter said, wrapping her

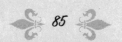

arms around herself as he slid on his helmet and started up the scooter.

And then, just as quickly as the day had passed, he was gone.

Carter was dying to talk to Rosie. But when she'd asked one of her attendants, she'd learned that Rosie was at yet another planning meeting, this time for the royal ball.

"Okay, thanks," Carter said, walking slowly down the corridor. She couldn't blame Rosie—she was the queen after all. And she had to be exhausted. But Carter was superexcited and needed someone to talk to. She didn't want to go back and hang out in her room alone. She just wanted a little company.

One of the servants was walking by and impulsively Carter called out, "Excuse me— do you know where Natalie is?"

The servant—a woman with curly blond hair and the greenest eyes Carter had ever seen looked nervous at the mention of Natalie's name.

"Well, miss, she sent her dinner back three times this evening and left the dining room hungry." The servant lowered her already quiet voice. "We decided to give her some space. When I last saw her she was on her way to her room."

"Mmmm. Thanks." Natalie's room was just down the hallway from Carter's. When Carter stopped beside Natalie's open door and didn't see the little princess, she got a funny feeling. Frowning, she started walking quickly down the palace corridor to her own room, her pace picking up as she rounded the corner.

When she arrived at her room, Carter hesitated at the sound of the television. She hadn't left it on, had she? She put her hand on the doorknob and pulled the door open.

The little nine-year-old princess was

going through her things.

She held up a turquoise plastic-framed photograph of Carter and her dad that Carter had stuck in her suitcase. They were standing in front of the lake wearing Bait Shack T-shirts covered with muck, shorts, and wading boots, a pile of largemouth bass displayed on a table behind them.

Natalie smiled at Carter like a cat that had just caught—and devoured—a canary. "Royalty? Not even close."

Chapter 7

Seeing someone going through your things without permission was pretty infuriating. But Carter was quickly learning that when they had something on you, it became infinitely worse.

"Did anyone ever teach you the meaning of privacy?" Carter stalked across the room and yanked the frame from Natalie's hands. She was more than a little aggravated.

"Did anyone teach you the meaning of honesty?" Natalie retorted, sitting cross-legged on the floor. She held up a Lake Monroe High School sweatshirt and Carter's math book. "You aren't a royal at all. You lied to me. That's the worst thing a friend can do—lie to someone."

"I—I—" Carter stopped, stuck on the word *friend*. Friend? Was that how Natalie really saw her? Carter swallowed. It was time for the whole truth.

"Natalie, you're right. I shouldn't have said I'm a royal. I'm not. That was just me being stupid. I'm just a friend of Rosie's." Once she started to talk, the words wouldn't stop. "I met Rosie when the Princess Protection Program sent her to Louisiana. Where I'm from."

Natalie's face scrunched up as if she was trying to make sense out of everything. "What do you know about the P.P.P.?" she asked guardedly, folding her arms in front of her chest.

"My dad is Major Mason. He works for them," Carter told her. "And when Ro—I mean Queen Rosalinda needed protection, they placed her with me and my dad back home in the United States."

"So you're like . . . a bodyguard?"

Carter laughed. "Nah. That's more my dad's style. I'm just a high school student. But," she said, bending down so she was eye-level with Natalie, "because of what Rosie and I went through together, we do have a little bit of experience with princesses going undercover."

"I knew you weren't really a royal," Natalie said with a sniff. "You just did way too many things wrong. No real princess would ever—"

Her words were cut short by a news bulletin that flashed on the TV. A reporter was standing on a busy European street corner, giving an update on Natalie's homeland.

"Things are heating up in the custody battle between Prince Robert and his former wife, Countess Lucienne." A series of photos of a serious looking middle-aged man, a pretty blond woman, and the biggest castle Carter had ever seen flashed on the screen. "At stake are not only Robert and Lucienne's four residences, nine automobiles, a royal yacht, and bank accounts that some estimates peg at two hundred fifty million dollars. But their most prized possession of all is Her Royal Highness, Princess Natalie." Footage played of a young Natalie taking her first steps, playing in a park, and attending a theater gala.

Carter stared at the screen. She couldn't imagine how hard it would be growing up in the spotlight.

The reporter looked grim. "Rumors have swirled for weeks that one of her parents might attempt to flee the country with Natalie. And making this situation even more peculiar? No one has seen the young princess in over a week."

"My mother and father wouldn't do anything to hurt me," Natalie declared, her chin trembling. "Mother says that the newspapers and magazines like to make up lies about people. They think it's entertainment." A tear slid down her cheek. "They don't understand that we're real people with feelings."

"I understand, Natalie," Carter said softly. "And you're right. Your parents would never do anything to hurt you. That's why they're working together with the P.P.P. The Princess Protection Program put you here in Costa Luna with Rosie because they knew you'd be in good hands."

"But I've been hanging out with you," Natalie pointed out. "An American teenager who said she was a royal."

As the reporter droned on about other rich kids caught in their parents' crossfire, Carter picked up the remote and clicked off the TV. "That's enough of that." Then she knelt alongside the little princess, trying to think of the right words to say.

The truth was, she was worried. Really worried. Natalie was bossy. Spoiled. Entitled. Indulged beyond belief.

But she was also really important to two people named Robert and Lucienne. Two people who loved her more than their entire fortunes. So much, in fact, that they'd sent her away for her own safety while they worked out their divorce. And that had to count for something.

Carter wished with every fiber of her being that they would get their acts together and realize that their daughter's future was at stake.

I mean, I've only known the pampered princess for a few days, and she's actually grown on me, she thought. If anything were to happen to Natalie while she was here in

Costa Luna, Carter wouldn't be able to forgive herself.

"I've got an idea," Carter began. "About the me being a royal thing. You like games, right?"

Natalie looked at her for a moment, then nodded.

"This is the coolest kind of game—one that has real life stakes, and one that only you and I can play," Carter said, warming to her words as she said them. "Andy thinks I'm a royal, right? So until I tell him I'm not—and I *will* tell him—I have to keep pretending." She took a deep, steadying breath. "And everyone at the palace thinks you're a commoner. So until it's safe to tell them you aren't, *you* need to keep pretending."

Natalie looked unsure.

"I had to do the same thing with Rosie," Carter confided. "Some really bad guys were after her when she was at my school, and

I had to pretend to be her in order to keep her safe."

"You did?" Natalie asked, wavering.

"Yep." Her identity switch had only lasted for a few minutes and she'd worn a mask, but Natalie didn't need to know that. Carter held her breath, hoping that her logic made some sense. If Natalie didn't go along with it, there was no telling the embarrassment she could face if the little princess came face-to-face with Andy.

Not that Carter had any idea whether or not she'd see him again—he said he'd call but that could just have been his way of saying *see ya*.

One thing was for sure: she was an idiot for not telling him the truth already.

A wave of relief washed over her when Natalie, her forehead furrowed, nodded. "Okay, Carter. Whatever you say."

Carter blinked. What was going on?

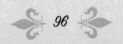

Natalie was totally giving in. She sees me as a princess-protection expert now, Carter realized. I'm not just some teenager telling her what to do.

A mischievous smile spread across Carter's face. "And as anyone knows, when you play a role, you've got to look the part." She jumped to her feet. "How do you feel about playing dress-up?"

One of the best rooms in the palace was also the smallest and messiest—royal dress-designer Mr. Elegante's workshop.

And in the past month, it had grown even messier. The designer was working day and night making costumes for the royal family to wear in the parade as well as a new ball gown for Rosie.

Tonight the workshop was quiet—Mr. Elegante was obviously taking a well-deserved night off. Dressmaker dummies with his latest creations stood in the middle of the room, and there were buttons, bows, sequins, palettes, and lots and lots of fabric and thread.

"Look," Natalie said breathily, pointing to an open box. Inside was the biggest emerald ring and earrings that Carter had ever seen. "I can't believe they left the royal jewels out."

Carter was surprised, too. "I guess they consider this a safe zone. They weren't counting on people like us coming in and trying them on." She put the heavy ring on her finger. "It doesn't even look real."

"I want to try that on," Natalie said, pointing to a pink feathered bolero that hung on a rack of garments. She slipped it over her thin shoulders. "How do I look?"

Carter picked up a jewel-encrusted scepter from a worktable and waved it over Natalie's head. "I crown thee Royal Ostrich," she said, laughing. The scepter was superheavy, and Carter couldn't even guess how much it was probably worth.

She put on a bright pink dress with a huge tulle skirt. "This dress should have a warning on it: the skirt is so wide it's bound to knock someone over."

"Oh, Carter." Natalie's hands were clasped to her chest. "That looks amazing on you! You must wear it to the ball. With this!" She picked up a diamond choker dripping with snowflakes made out of rubies.

What would Andy think if he saw me in this? Carter mused, putting the necklace on. What would my friends back home think?

They'd think she won the lottery—or lost her mind.

"And this is so you," Carter said, sliding a stack of sparkling bangles onto Natalie's arm. Really, Carter thought, you'd think a palace would do a better job of keeping their precious jewels under wraps.

"I'm so sure, darling," Natalie said, tossing back her hair. She began walking across the room like a model on a catwalk. "Charmed, I'm sure."

They were just in the middle of a fierce sword fight with scepters—heavier, but much more dramatic than pool noodles— when the workshop door swung open.

Carter's heart was in her throat as she clutched the scepter to her pink beaded bodice. Mr. Elegante?

Not quite. Rosie leaned against the doorframe, giggling. "If I'd known you were playing princess, I would have skipped out of my meeting an hour ago."

Chapter

8

"Please, Miss Mason, you must stand still." Mr. Elegante, pins held between his lips, pulled back and gave Carter an appraisal. "Almost, my dear. We just need a little more ruche on the left."

"My feelings exactly," Carter said, blowing a piece of hair off her face. She had no idea what ruche was. Or dolman sleeves, flounced hems, or illusion bodices. Dress-making was like a foreign language—and only Mr. Elegante and Rosie spoke it.

It was early the next morning, and she, Rosie, and Natalie were all being fitted for their ball gowns. Carter stood in the middle of the workshop on a circular dais as Mr. Elegante moved around her, pinning, tucking, and marking the custom pale peach dress she would be wearing—a surprise gift from Rosie. Mr. Elegante hummed as he worked.

"I don't know how you stand this all the time, Rosie," Carter said, then shot a guilty look at Mr. Elegante. "No offense."

Rosie shrugged. She was sitting in a Louis XVI chair, her dainty feet resting on an ottoman. Mr. Elegante had been working for weeks on her dress, and today was just a matter of checking the hemline. The queen's gown hung on a padded hanger, ready for the royal ball tomorrow. Now all she had to do was offer her opinion on the dresses for Carter and Natalie. "I am used to it, I suppose. And Mr. Elegante has never let me down."

"It helps to have such wonderful beauty to work with," Mr. Elegante said with a low bow. He finished up with Carter and moved on to Natalie, who was eyeing the feather bolero from last night.

"No no, my dear," he said when she begged him to let her wear it. "That is not the look we want for our beautiful nine-year-old guest."

"How about this?" Natalie suggested, pulling a purple lamé dress off the rack.

"That's for when you're mad at Rosie, right?" Carter cracked. It wasn't just lamé . . . it was *lame*.

"Different occasions require different types of dresses," Mr. Elegante murmured, always the diplomat.

"Then this," Natalie announced. She held up another dress—this one a red sequin number—that was a definite DON'T.

Rosie shook her head. "No, Natalie. That is not right for you." She thought for a moment, then got up and walked over to Mr. Elegante's armoire. "I seem to remember

some beautiful blue chiffon we wanted to use for one of my state-dinner dresses, but did not have enough to make it work. But for a child . . ." She opened the armoire doors and pulled out a puffy bolt of shimmering sky blue fabric.

"Magnifique!" Natalie squealed, running over to touch it. She gazed up at Carter, eyes shining. "It's just like the sparkle fairy's dress in *Fairy Butterfly Sparkles!*"

Carter held her palms up. "And really, who could ask for more?"

Then, to her surprise, she heard her cell phone vibrate in her bag.

"I'll get it!" Natalie yelped, diving for the phone. She flipped it open. "It's him! BSBLLFN57! He wants to know if you're free for dinner tonight. Are you?"

"Am I?" Carter asked Rosie, lifting an eyebrow.

"Is she?" Natalie chimed in.

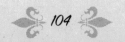

Mr. Elegante let out a small cough. "There is a lovely ruffled skirt just waiting to be worn."

Rosie smiled. "I think you are most definitely free, Carter."

Natalie looked at Carter, wide-eyed. "And I know where you should eat. Here!"

"In the workshop?" Mr. Elegante asked, frowning.

"No—at the palace! He thinks you're a royal anyway."

Now Mr. Elegante looked thoroughly confused.

"Bad idea," Carter said, shaking her head so emphatically that three pins fell off her dress. "It was awkward enough when he dropped me off in front of the palace. No way am I going to bring him inside."

Carter could only imagine the embarrassing situations she could end up in—she could never ever pull off being a member of the royal family here, in front of the *real* royal family. And if I tell Andy the truth, he'll think I'm such a jerk, she thought.

"I just got swept up in that lie, and . . . and I liked him too much to risk telling him who I really am," she mumbled, shoulders dropping.

"Carter, it is better to tell him the truth. If he is as nice as you have told me, he will understand. Everyone makes mistakes," Rosie told her sympathetically. "And besides, you will have privacy here."

"He's very dreamy," Natalie said, batting her eyelashes. "He looks like Evan, the bass player from the Reynolds Three—they performed at my birthday party. Except Andy has curlier hair."

"A curly-haired Evan Reynolds . . . I see what the fuss is about," Rosie said, her eyes twinkling. She held up a finger as Carter started to protest. "Seriously, Carter, I feel terrible that I've had to spend so much time working during your visit. I'm excited that you have met someone to show you around."

"Please do it, Carter. Please?" Natalie begged. "I promise I won't get in your way. Or—or do anything you'd be mad at me for."

"Well . . ." Carter really wasn't crazy about the idea. But if she was ever going to tell Andy the truth, now—and here—was as good a time and place as any. "Fine. Give me my phone."

She punched in a text.

baitgirl: gr8. how abt at the palace. 6?

bsbllfn57: :)

"Now, Mr. Elegante," she said as he threaded a needle, "about that skirt . . ."

Chapter
9

*W*aiting around for six o'clock to arrive was going to be torture if Carter didn't come up with something to take her mind off things. Not only did she have the normal jitters about spending time with a cool new guy that she really liked—she was going to have to tell him that she hadn't been upfront about who she was.

Rosie had headed into Pamalisah with some of her staff. They were going to meet with local officials and discuss the parade route and other logistics.

"You need to tell me everything when I get back," she told Carter before she left.

"And remember, Carter. If he's as great as you think he is, he's going to understand why you did what you did." Rosie had also let Carter know that he would be a welcome guest at the royal ball—if she wanted to ask him.

Did she? She'd have to see how the night went.

So, with Natalie under her care until five, when the cook promised to step in, Carter had decided they would take a walk around the palace grounds. Rosie had given her a map, marking the must-see spots with red Xs.

"You actually have a map of your backyard," Carter had said, shaking her head.

Now that they'd started walking, Carter could see why a map was necessary. The palace grounds were beautifully landscaped with shrubs, bushes, and flowering trees and seemed to spread out for miles.

"Hello," Natalie said cheerfully to a gardener trimming a hedge with a giant pair of clippers. "Enjoy your day!"

Someone woke up on the right side of her king-size bed, Carter thought, surprised. She hoped the good attitude would last.

Along the pathway were flowers of every size and color—roses, tulips, and others Carter had never seen before. Ornamental shrubs and bushes grew in manicured lines, and benches dotted the landscape.

"Let's visit the manmade lake," Natalie suggested, pointing to an X on the map.

"Okay," Carter agreed.

The lake was just a short walk away, and they had to cross over a small pedestrian bridge that was guarded by a palace security gate.

When they arrived at the lake, they saw that they weren't alone—a large tour group was making its way along, led by an official palace attendant in uniform. The tourists were snapping pictures and thumbing through their guidebooks as the attendant gave a brief history of the lake.

Rosie had told Carter that although the palace was closed to the public, they did open part of the palace grounds for guided tours. "It would be a shame not to share the beauty of these grounds with the people of my country," she had explained.

The lake was like a mirror, reflecting the trees and flowers on its glossy surface. Natalie skipped over to a small tourist cart that sold bottled water and roasted nuts. "May I get something?" she asked Carter.

Carter's face fell. "Sorry, Natalie, I didn't bring any cash." She braced herself for the whining that was sure to follow.

But instead of getting upset, Natalie smiled. "I wouldn't dream of asking you to pay, Carter. I have my own." She took out a

tiny leather purse shaped like a hippo, shook out some coins, and bought two waters.

"Thank you, sir," she said, as the vendor handed over two icy cold bottles. "Here you are, Carter. My treat."

Carter took the bottle and stared down at the little princess. "Strange . . . I didn't see the alien spaceship come down and replace the old Natalie with this new-and-improved one." She was like a different person.

Natalie peeked up at Carter and let out a giggle. "You're funny, Carter."

"No, seriously. What gives?"

The little princess looked down at her sneakers. "I know that I wasn't exactly acting like a princess, Carter. I just—I just like to see what I can get away with." She shrugged.

Carter laughed. Natalie was a little con artist!

"And I liked that you didn't let me get

away with anything," Natalie continued, looking kind of embarrassed. "Sometimes I do stuff like that back home. The servants who do everything I ask them to do—they never end up staying."

"And the ones who don't wait on you hand and foot?" Carter prompted.

"I like them the best," Natalie confessed. "Then I know they're not just being nice to me because I'm a royal. It can get kind of boring always getting your way." She hesitated. "That's why I like you, Carter. You're real."

Carter felt her cheeks flush at the unexpected compliment. It was really sweet. "That's very nice of you, Natalie," she told the little princess. "I appreciate that." Funny enough, Carter saw a lot of herself in Natalie. She was kind of like that, too, when it came to people—challenging them was a kind of test to see if they were worthy of her friendship. She was developing a real soft spot for the little kid.

"And because you're so real, I know that you'll say yes to what I'm about to ask you."

Carter gave her a dubious look. "And what's that?"

Natalie giggled. "If I can join you and Andy tonight on your date."

Okay. The girl wasn't just a con artist— she was a master manipulator in training.

"Uh . . . no," she told Natalie, who looked crestfallen. "But nice try."

"Please Carter? Pretty please? I promise I'll be good."

Carter wasn't about to cave. "No dice, lady. But think of it this way. You might not be getting what you want." She grinned. "But you know for sure that I like you."

"This is the state room, where they do all sorts of state things. And the map room—

definitely where you want to head if you're lost." Carter walked hurriedly down the palace corridor, Andy jogging after her to keep up.

At 5:55, Carter had still been trying to decide what to wear. She'd finally chosen the cotton ruffled skirt that Mr. Elegante had mentioned and paired it with her own cotton tee and a pair of flip-flops. When a servant had knocked on the door to say that her guest had arrived, she had to swallow the cold hard lump of nervousness that had lodged in her throat.

This was it. The moment of truth. She didn't know why she was beating herself up over this, really. It wasn't like she was going to be seeing Andy after the week was over. He didn't go to her school—or even live in the United States! Once they said good-bye, that would be it.

I guess I just don't want to leave him

with a horrible impression of American girls. Me, in particular, she thought.

Carter brushed her hair one last time and put on some pink lip gloss. He was going to get the real Carter Mason tonight. Hopefully he'd like her as much as the "royal" one.

Now, as the two of them walked through the palace hallways, Carter found herself walking fast and talking faster. She had a terrible habit of talking really quickly when she got nervous—and right now her words were coming out like machine-gun fire.

Andy looked really cute tonight. He wore pressed khaki pants, a white dress shirt, and black leather loafers. Carter realized it was because he was at the palace, and not necessarily to impress her. Still, he didn't seem all that curious or intimidated about being in the Royal Palace of Costa Luna. It was as if he'd strolled down the palace hallways a thousand times.

I guess material things don't really impress him, she thought. And that made Carter like him even more.

"Kitchen, office, office, family room that seats thirty," Carter rattled off.

"I'm thinking maybe you shouldn't go back to the United States. You'd make a great palace tour guide here in Costa Luna," Andy said, stopping to touch a marble bust of some old guy wearing a George Washington–style wig.

"I'll have to consider that," Carter said. "Keep my options open."

He gazed around. "Is Queen Rosalinda here tonight?"

Carter shook her head. "She's busy getting everything ready for Independence Day. I'm sure she'd have loved to have said hello. She's been, um, really gracious to me."

He nodded. "That would have been cool to have met her."

Carter shrugged. "Well, you know, you meet one queen, you meet them all." She gave an inward shudder. What on earth was she talking about?

"You never told me exactly what kind of royal you are, Carter," Andy said, as they pushed open a set of French doors and walked out onto a grand terrace. "I don't know a lot about American history, but I do know that you don't have a monarchy."

Carter let out a nervous chuckle. "Just Hollywood royalty," she babbled, "and, well, hmmm. You know." Suddenly she was horribly tongue-tied. Gorgeous setting, perfect weather, cute guy—and a sick feeling in the pit of her stomach.

He was giving her what she needed—the perfect opportunity to make things right.

But she couldn't bring herself to tell him

the truth. What if he storms off? What if he thinks I'm a lunatic? What if—what if—

Andy reached for her hand, startling her from her thoughts. "Beautiful."

"I know. Isn't it amazing?" Carter said, gazing at the view off the terrace, and happy that he'd changed the subject.

"I wasn't talking about the view." Andy leaned over and gave her a quick kiss on the cheek. "Now. What's that you were telling me earlier about a dinner on the beach?"

Waves lapped the shore, sending sand crabs scurrying. Carter sat back on the plaid blanket, resting her weight on her hands. The cook had packed a picnic dinner for her and Andy, and as they shared bread, cheese, ham, fruit, and sparkling grape juice, they'd had great conversation. Andy was so easy to talk to. It was as if they'd known each other forever.

He also had endless good-natured patience. Because after they'd discovered Natalie spying on them from behind a huge boulder, Andy hadn't gotten mad. Instead, he had asked the little princess to join them! Now Andy and Natalie were running up and down the small private beach, laughing and playing tag with the water.

I should have known Natalie wouldn't take no for answer, Carter thought, ticked off. She wasn't at all fine with what was going on—but she didn't want to look bad in front of Andy by making Natalie leave.

And besides, Natalie knows the truth. If I make her mad, she might blab to Andy before I can tell him.

"Come on, Carter! Catch us!" Natalie shouted, sticking out her tongue.

"Yeah, catch us!" Andy called, waving his arms.

Brushing the sand from her legs, Carter

got up and started chasing them. Maybe tossing the little princess in the waves wouldn't be such a bad idea.

Squealing, Natalie darted off behind another cluster of boulders. And Andy was just too fast. Every time Carter got near him, he darted the opposite way, his eyes dancing.

"You aren't giving up yet," he teased as she stopped to catch her breath. "Or maybe it's time I chased you."

"No!" Carter shrieked, taking off in the opposite direction from Natalie. Seconds later she felt Andy's hands on her waist. He turned her around so that she was facing him.

"You're very cute when you run," he teased, sliding his arms around her. "Frankly, you're very cute all the time."

Carter's pulse was racing—from the chase and her nerves. "Gee, thanks," was all

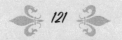

she could manage. She wanted to tell him how cute he was, too. But she was sure that at any moment Natalie's little blond head would pop up—maybe even in between them. Time was running out.

"Um, Andy?" Carter said, staring up into his warm, kind eyes. "I—"

"Hey, guys! I found a hermit crab!" Natalie's voice carried across the breeze. "Come look!"

"We're coming!" Andy shouted to her, then looked back at Carter. "Sorry—what were you saying?"

Carter gathered her courage. Even if she only had time for a few words, she didn't have a choice. It was now or never.

"Would you want to go to the royal ball with me?" she blurted out, digging her toes into the sand.

He smiled, then kissed her on the lips.

I guess that's a yes, she thought, smiling.

Chapter 10

*A*fter all the preparations—the meetings, the e-mails, the long phone calls—the event Rosie had anticipated ever since she was crowned queen had arrived in Costa Luna! The annual Independence Day festivities kicked off with a grand parade through the streets of downtown Pamalisah.

Bands marched, flag twirlers twirled, antique cars decorated with flowers cruised, floats floated—and the best part of all was that the weather had cooperated: it was sunny, not too warm, and not too chilly. Simply perfect.

Rosie smoothed the white satin skirt of

her new ball gown and waved to her people from the open window of her antique horse-drawn carriage. The glossy black coach trimmed with gold was pulled by two beautiful white horses.

She had perfected the royal wave: fore-arm held upright, hand swishing from side to side like a windshield wiper. Her mother, Sophia, sat next to her, looking elegant in her purple cocktail dress, her hair swept up.

"Your father would be so proud of you, Rosalinda," Sophia told her, tears of joy welling up in her eyes. "This is a day he dreamed of for many, many years."

Rosie nodded, stopping her constant wave to squeeze her mother's hand. "I hope to always make him—and you—proud, Mama."

"The look in your people's eyes is your answer, *m'ija*," her mother said, smiling at the throngs of Costa Lunans who had gathered. "People throughout Costa Luna celebrate our country and you today!"

Sophia was not exaggerating. Everywhere Rosie could see, there were people. Standing on sidewalks, sitting in folding chairs and on the curb, waving from rooftops and windows. Rosie swelled with pride. It was so exciting to see people dressed in the colors of Costa Luna—red and purple—and waving the Costa Lunan flag. She spotted a group of teenagers with their hair dyed purple—and lots of children with their faces painted.

"Hello! Hello!" she called out, smiling from ear to ear. When the parade had first started, Rosie had been thinking about all the things that needed to happen and making last minute phone calls. Then, her mother had said, "Rosalinda. It is done. The day you have worked so hard for is here. No more worrying or planning—just enjoy."

And what made this special day even better was that earlier that morning, Rosie had received a call from the Director of the Princess Protection Program. The de Rouens had come to their senses and worked out the details of their custody arrangement in an amicable, friendly manner. Things were looking very positive for Natalie to reunite with her parents very soon.

Rosie waved to an elderly couple holding hands and a couple of children who shrieked, "We love you, Queen Rosalinda!" as her coach passed.

"I love you, too!" she called.

"Over there! Over there!" Natalie crowed, pointing to a cluster of boys excitedly waving Costa Lunan flags.

Carter reached into the huge sack beside her and threw a handful of candy in their direction.

She and Natalie were riding on a huge float covered with flowers. Tall maypoles decorated with streamers and more flowers were scattered around them. Their float was behind a terrific marching band wearing white pants and purple jackets, and in front of a group of miniature horses, which were guaranteed crowd-pleasers. Rosie's carriage was several spots ahead.

The parade was televised, so Natalie wore a gypsy costume, complete with emerald green harem pants and a veil over her face, to make sure that no one would recognize her. Carter had on a similar outfit in yellow.

"Can I throw some candy?" Natalie asked, her small hand hovering over the sack.

"Sure. Just make sure you don't hit anyone!" Carter cautioned, waving to the crowd.

Natalie tossed a handful of caramels to a group of squealing kids. "Rosie told me that today, everyone is Costa Lunan. Even me!"

Carter nodded happily as a troop of dancing clowns ran past their float, squirting water out of lapel-pin flowers and making the crowd laugh.

I wonder if Andy's somewhere out there, she thought, shielding her eyes from the sun as she gazed across the cheering crowd. If he was, Carter hoped that he was having a great time, too.

And that he's still in a good mood when I tell him the truth at the ball tonight, she thought nervously.

"I didn't know you were such a good dancer," Carter complimented Mr. Elegante as they exited the dance floor.

He gave a slight bow. "And you should see my cha-cha. Now, please, Miss Mason—

the skirt on your dress is made for twirling. Don't disappoint me."

Carter gave the royal dress designer a warm smile as he headed off into the crowd in search of a new waltz partner.

"Punch, miss?" a server asked, handing her a glass filled with a frothy pink liquid.

"Oh. Thanks." Carter took a sip and looked around the grand ballroom. Crystal chandeliers bathed the room with soft, romantic light, and cascading lilies and orchids framed the many archways carved into the stucco walls. She'd taken a few pictures to show people back home.

Where is Andy? Carter thought, taking a peek at the clock on her cell. He had said he'd meet her at eight o'clock in the entry-way to the grand ballroom. When he hadn't shown by eight fifteen, Carter sent a quick text:

baitgirl: whr r u?

There was still no response. Being alone at the ball was starting to make her feel a little self-conscious and even more nervous. Had Andy discovered the truth about her? Was that why he hadn't shown up yet?

Rosie, her mother, some royal relatives, and important government officials were having photographs taken in the Aspen Room. Natalie was twirling with a smiling Henri on the dance floor.

And here I am, fighting down butterflies, Carter said to herself. She shook her head and took another slow sip of her punch. At first she'd just been anxious about what she was going to say to him. That anxiety, though, had been replaced by worries that maybe she wasn't even going to see Andy before she left. She was flying back to her real life the next day.

Then, someone at the far end of the room caught her attention. Someone in a tux with a big grin on his face was waving.

"You made it," Carter said, walking over to him. Her heart thumped in time to the music.

"Wow. You look amazing," Andy said, stepping back to look at her. He leaned over and gave her a kiss on the cheek.

"I have to tell you something and it can't wait any longer." She took a steadying gulp of air. "I'm not a member of the royal family—here in Costa Luna or anywhere. I'm just a completely normal, regular girl. Natalie was bugging me, and I lied and told her I was a royal. But then when she told you that, I was embarrassed—and I just couldn't tell you it wasn't true. And then I got to know you and started liking you, and then I definitely couldn't tell you the truth." She took another gulp. "But I'm telling you the truth now."

Andy just stared at her.

"Do—can you forgive me?" she croaked. "I mean, I understand if you—"

To her utter amazement, Andy took both her hands in his . . . and started laughing. Really laughing.

"No offense, Carter, but I had a feeling you weren't exactly being honest about your, uh, royal roots."

Carter felt her face flushing. "Was it that obvious?" she moaned.

"And when you didn't show up in the Aspen Room, it was pretty much confirmed." He squeezed her hands. "But, I wasn't hanging out with you because you were supposedly a royal. I just thought you seemed like a cool girl and wanted to get to know you better."

"The Aspen Room? Why were you in the Aspen Room?" she asked, her mind racing. "Are *you* a royal?"

Andy nodded, his brown eyes twinkling.

"That's what it says on my birth certificate."

Carter put her hands on his chest and gave him a shove. "Shut up!" All this time she'd been worried about pretending to be someone she wasn't—and Andy was an undercover . . . duke? Lord? *Prince?*

"My father was a distant cousin of Roberto, the late king's father," Andy said by way of explanation. "So I am, by birth, a royal."

"I wish you would have told me," Carter said, looking up at him. "It would have made these last few days a whole lot less stressful."

"No stress," Andy told her, taking her hand. "Tonight is about having fun."

Andy led Carter out onto the dance floor and they joined the crowd in a waltz. One dance turned into two and then six. Carter smiled up at Andy the whole time, her skirt swirling around them, her heart skipping a beat every time Andy smiled back at her.

"How about some punch?" Andy said when the last song ended.

Carter nodded and, holding Andy's hand tightly, followed him off the dance floor.

They stood on the edge of the crowd, sipping punch and watching the elegant dancers. Carter was amazed at the entire evening—Rosie's work had certainly paid off, and things with Andy were . . . incredible. She felt a pang of regret that she'd be on a plane home tomorrow.

Andy took the empty punch glass from her hand and set it on a servant's tray. "Shall we?" he asked, his eyes twinkling.

Carter smiled and took Andy's hand. Tomorrow was still hours away.

"Carter?" Queen Rosalinda, accompanied by several attendants, had materialized at Carter and Andy's side. She looked down at Carter's fingers, entwined with Andy's.

"*This* is your mystery man?" she blurted

out as the band struck up a new song. "You mean your Andy is . . . *Andreas*? My little cousin?"

"That's right," Andy replied before whirling a giggling Carter out on to the dance floor and winking at an astonished Rosie. "And it's clear your friend has excellent taste."

"You didn't have to come," Carter told Andy the next afternoon. They stood on the windy tarmac beside a sleek private jet. A black sedan was parked several hundred yards away from them. Rosie had arranged for the jet to fly Carter home. "But I'm glad you did."

"Are you kidding? I wouldn't miss the chance to see you one more time." He stuck his hands in his pockets. "Now you promise you're going to stay in touch, right?"

"I promise." Carter smiled.

They'd danced, laughed, and hung out with Rosie and the palace staffers until the wee hours of the morning. Carter even got the chance to meet some of Andy's friends, and they were all really cool. It was a night Carter would never forget.

She and Andy had agreed that it wasn't realistic to think they'd have a long-distance romance. But Andy had promised that she'd always have a burger-loving, baseball-fanatic friend in Costa Luna that she could count on any time. And Carter had made him promise that if he ever came to the United States, he'd include a stop in Lake Monroe, Louisiana.

"And I'm glad you finally decided to let me know who you really are," Andy whispered, tucking a piece of Carter's hair behind her ear. "A really special girl."

Carter closed her eyes as Andy gave her a sweet good-bye kiss.

The car door opened, and Natalie came bounding out, with Rosie several steps behind her. "Good-bye, Carter," Natalie said, throwing her arms around her. She wore a pair of jeans and a T-shirt that said *Princess Power*. Her blond hair was pulled back in a butterfly-shaped ponytail holder. "I can't wait to tell Mother and Father about you." She pulled back to look up at her. "Maybe you could be my new nanny!"

Carter, Andy, and Rosie started laughing. "That's very sweet—and very tempting," Carter said. "I wish I could."

"I thought you were all about being honest," Rosie teased as Natalie bounded back toward the car.

"She's a cute kid," Carter said with a smile. She gave Andy one last hug, and with a wave, he jogged back to the car so that she and Rosie could have a private good-bye.

"I know you must be very sad to say

farewell to Andreas," Rosie said, concerned.

Carter sighed. "He's really cool. And so cute. But I can deal." She grinned. "And Rosie? He's so not an Andreas."

Rosie smiled. "I will make sure that you and *Andy* see each other again. And that, next time, you and I will spend more time together."

"We said that last time," Carter reminded her, thinking of when they were in Washington, D.C., for Rosie's first official state visit. "But don't worry about it. You threw the most awesome party this country has ever seen. I'm just glad I got the chance to be here."

Rosie put her arms around Carter and gave her best friend a hug. "Thank you, Carter. It was fun, wasn't it?"

"The best," Carter declared. "And the next time we get together, we're going to work on a boy for you."

"Any cute relatives in the Mason family I should know about?" Rosie asked with a giggle, her long hair blowing in the wind.

Carter nodded. "Well, my cousin Matthew is quite the ladies man . . . at his preschool."

The airplane door opened, and a smiling flight attendant curtsied at the sight of Rosie. "Your Highness. Miss Mason, the pilot has asked that you come aboard so we can prepare for departure."

"Thanks so much, Rosie," Carter said, giving her friend one last hug before heading up the stairs to the jet. "I had a really great time."

"I am glad, Carter. And I hope that the gift that is waiting for you on the plane will always remind you that you are welcome here anytime." Rosie smiled. "Now go."

baitgirl: is this real????

hrhqueenrosalinda: Yes.

baitgirl: r u kidding?

hrhqueenrosalinda: No! :)

baitgirl: i luv it!!!! tx!!!!!!! ttyl!

Carter turned off her phone as the plane began taxiing down the runway. She removed a sparkling amethyst-and-ruby locket from a black velvet box—purple and red jewels for the colors of Costa Luna—and fastened it around her neck. Inside were two photos—one of her and Rosie, and one of her and Andy last night at the ball.

I am the luckiest girl ever, Carter thought, leaning back in her soft leather seat and gazing out into the clear blue sky.

She would never, ever pretend to be someone she wasn't ever again. Being

Carter Mason was just too good.

Unless the Princess Protection Program needed her help.

And then—all bets were off.

But the necklace from her BFF? That was definitely staying on.

Don't miss the next book in the Princess
Protection Program series

Top Secret TIARAS

By Wendy Loggia

Based on "Princess Protection Program," Teleplay by Annie De Young

Based on the Story by David Morgasen and Annie De Young

*C*arter Mason and Queen Rosalinda are in
for more excitement and adventure! Rosie's
attending a royal summit and Carter gets to tag
along. When an old friend—a cute prince—tells
her that two princesses, who have been feuding
since the summit began, are in danger, Rosie
and Carter are on high alert. And when one of
the princesses goes missing, the two friends set
out to find her.